True Worthy Hoit, J. M. Toner Collection

The Model Man

An oration on Washington, in which he is compared with the sages and

heroes of antiquity

True Worthy Hoit, J. M. Toner Collection

The Model Man
An oration on Washington, in which he is compared with the sages and heroes of antiquity

ISBN/EAN: 9783337195885

Printed in Europe, USA, Canada, Australia, Japan

Cover: Foto ©Andreas Hilbeck / pixelio.de

More available books at **www.hansebooks.com**

THE MODEL MAN:

AN ORATION ON

WASHINGTON,

IN WHICH

HE IS COMPARED WITH THE SAGES AND HEROES OF ANTIQUITY,
TOGETHER WITH AN ANALYSIS OF HIS CHARACTER,
AND THE ANNUNCIATION OF HIM AS THE
MODEL MAN.

BY

T. W. HOIT,

President of the Saint Louis Literary and Philosophical Association.

THIS CELEBRATED ORATION IS PUBLISHED AND FOR SALE BY PUBLISHERS
AND AGENTS THROUGHOUT THE UNITED STATES AND EUROPE.

———— • ————

ST. LOUIS. MO.:
1866.

Printed by T. W. Ustick, 79 Locust Street.

PREFACE.

The purpose of the author of the following Oration, is to hold up the character of WASHINGTON to the gaze of mankind as worthy of imitation. This is no original idea. Do we not know that the habitual contemplation of an admirable object makes a lasting and salutary impression on the mind? To be like Washington should be the desire and study of every American, and of every man. He is our ideal man. The qualities of his great soul render his fame enduring, and constitute the glory of human character : and the habitual contemplation of him, will tend to elevate and ennoble mankind.

There would seem to be little need of cultivating a love and veneration of this great man, since his name is on every tongue, and his fame is as broad as the earth : but the sun is often obscured by mist, and sometimes by dark clouds and tempests. What with the mysticism of our theologies, the dark clouds of superstition, and the raging storm of partisanism and sectional strife, there seems of late somewhat of a declension in public as well as individual patriotism, and a subsidence of our zeal for justice, freedom and equality. There is a worship of strange and false gods going on among us. The worship of them is inadequate to our wants as freemen. Mammon is one of these, and lo, his myriad slaves ! Another is an ideal tyrant.

filled with revenge and ire, in whose name mental
shackles are forged, and lo, the mind in chains! And
the gods of combat, and of love, and their shrines of
ambition and of pleasure, see blaze, with the unhallowed
flames of glory and of lust!

Turn from them, O children of freedom, turn, and
contemplate the nobler embodiment of human perfect-
ability in the mild, but august, aspect of our mighty
Washington. Brother, dost thou lack virtue? behold
it in him! Dost thou lack courage? his character
affords a supply! Dost thou lack wisdom? thou
mayest learn of him!

In the temple of Freedom there is room for all.
Truth welcomes all of you, my brothers, as votaries at
her shrine. Are some of you bound in sectarian
fetters? snap those fetters and be free. Behold in
Washington the mightiest work of an Almighty hand!
On you, Americans, I call: torn by faction, blinded,
some of you, by bigotry, tempted by both spiritual and
temporal foes, do you not see that your wants are
greater than these antiquated systems can supply?
What hope have we for the stability of republicanism
resting upon the basis of a superstition whose fun-
damental principle is despotism? What hope of
immortality and glory can we reasonably indulge, if
our mental eyes are blinded by mysticism, or dimmed
by the paraphernalia of these theological systems? The
sinless soul can see its God, by looking through nature
up to Him. Let us then admire his noblest work, and
honor the Maker in our admiration.

Europeans! Englishmen, Frenchmen, Germans,
Sclavonians, Australasians, on you I call. Leave your
dumb idols and behold the Model! Your first allegiance
is due to Him who created and sustains you, not to
your kings, nor through them. Your admiration is

due to the most beautiful work of His hand. Your
veneration is due to His wisdom reflected in the wisest
and greatest of mankind. Obey this summons and be
free. Acting thus, your minds will be free. And
freedom from your temporal shackles will thus
ultimately be attained.

Englishmen! ye elder brothers of Columbia, bright
daughter of Freedom, who has been the guardian angel
of your dreams for a thousand years, behold her
Model Son! copy him. Advance one step further and
be free. Frenchmen! have you forgotten the declara-
tion of your great warrior after the battle of Rivoli, that
" *none but* REPUBLICAN *troops could have fought with
such valor?*" The genius of your country is republican
still; our Model is for you. Germans! come to the
shrine of Freedom, come. Let your thronging millions
gladden these Western plains with anthems of freedom.
Behold this Model! copy it and be true men. Nors-
men, your sturdy frames and iron sinews are strong
for the ultimate right. Look hither, to the westward,
and behold the moral Colossus who overshadows your
model king. Australians, vassals of our former foe, do
ye already tire under the incubus of Albion? Follow
our example, behold our Model and copy it, until
Freedom shall vouchsafe to you a model of your own.

Washington is the embodiment of a new dispensa-
tion, wherein the ultimate of human progress is
prefigured, and the shining qualities of virtue, wisdom
and heroism, sagacity, moderation and energy, are
found just equipoise, and in which the measure of
faith, and the intensity of hope, are bounded and
regulated by probability, and veneration is justified by
the *quality* as well as the magnitude of that which is
to be revered. This is the character which challenges
the admiration of human reason, and is not repugnant

to it.   So far, then, it is new at least, for the old ideals
confounded reason and denied the just prerogative of
the mind, which makes it the arbiter of its own destiny,
by its assertion of the right of private judgment.

There is a latent, though powerful principle of the
human mind, which is summoned and aroused at this
ideal Washington, when contemplated as the Model
Man.   This principle results from the confluence, in
the mind, of veneration, love, gratitude, patriotism,
and admiration, and cannot be repressed by all the
force of dogmatic theology, nor diverted permanently
into foreign channels. It is the spontaneous and
legitimate response of mankind to the noblest of infinite
creations, and to suppress it would be to contempt-
uously mock at the mandate of Omnipotence. Is
there no meaning in the character of Washington?
Is there no significance in such an exhibition of Divine
Wisdom? If a sparrow falls not to the ground without
His notice, how can a Washington be seen but as a
glorious exhibition of Eternal Wisdom and Power.
Surely, he must be the Example for man to copy,
the necessity for which existed in the lack of faith in
earlier examples, and their inapplicability to man's
wants on account of his inability to follow in their
footsteps. Infidelity to other ideals may and does
exist, but infidelity to the character and principles of
Washington, is to be false to justice, truth and human
equality. The World expects Americans to be like
Washington.

If the comparisons instituted in this Oration, seem
to be invidious, let it be remembered that the object in
making them is not to eulogize the sages and heroes of
antiquity, but to show their inferiority to Washington.
This could only be done by pointing out their defects,
errors and misfortunes. The task of doing justice to

their virtues, I leave mainly to others, who have perhaps amply performed that pleasing duty already. As for the vices, errors and misfortunes of Washington, I aver he had none, whilst the task of adequately extolling his virtues is so great, that whatever of eulogy, or praise, or attempted hyperbole the past or the present may employ, that task must remain unperformed, because, to do justice to the character of Washington, he must be comprehended and appreciated, and to do this, we must be like him, which we may at most hope to be. His character, though real, seems ideal, and is so to us, because, though conceivable it is not attainable, and its reality cannot be arrived at by ocular demonstration. To *approximate* the character of Washington, therefore, is all that can reasonably be hoped for, and this is the proper development of man. It is the just development of the whole man.

I offer no apology for pointing out Washington as the Model Man. Our analysis of his character, shows that, on the whole, what is true of him, is true of no other man of ancient or modern times. His character as a human being challenges my entire admiration, and as an evidence of my sincerity in confidently commending the world to him, I would say to my children, as the last, best advice I would give them, study his character well and endeavor to be like Washington.

WASHINGTON

AND THE HEROES OF ANTIQUITY.

It is not becoming in us to say common things of the character of Washington. He is the principal figure in the picture of our time. Whatever of grandeur belongs to our country, it is only accessory in this picture. This broad continent, whose states are empires, whose plains are boundless, whose mountains overtop the clouds, whose far reaching rivers, and awful inland oceans, that roll, not to waft plenty from favored to deficient climes, but to combine variety and beauty with magnificence, and strike the mind with admiration and wonder, and whose cataracts resound the eternal anthem of freedom, form but the perspective which nature had drawn, as fitting scenery to adorn this stage of action, whereon is to be enacted the world's drama, in which we behold, conspicuous, this Great Actor, whose exploits command the world's applause. We behold the fadeless wreath of laurel placed upon his brow, to crown with immortal honor his actions, which realize the poetic idea of those Grecian and Trojan Heroes, whose allies were the immortal gods, by whose aid they were invincible. That which makes his exploits greater than theirs, is to be estimated by the difference between the deities of mythology and our God. His was a charmed life, while they were exposed to the vicissitudes of common mortals. Behold divine Petrocles

rall by the hand of Hector; Achilles rifled of his lawful spoils
of beauty, the loved Chryseis, and Ulysses and his companions
subjected to the vicissitudes of war, and

> "Wandering still from coast to coast,
> And all his vessels, all his people lost."

Lo! Hector, the Trojan, favorite of the gods, torn by the fate
of war from the fair Andromache and his infant son Astyanax;
see him slain by the fierce Achilles, his godlike form prone in
the dust, and at the chariot of the victor, dragged around the
walls of Troy.   And Achilles himself slain by the hand of
Paris.   This was the fate of the Grecian and Trojan Heroes,
but such is not the fate of Washington.   He fought to avenge
no private wrong, but to uphold the liberties of his country,
and for the enfranchisement of a world.   He was left to no
chances betwixt contending deities, nor governed by their
caprices, nor flattered by their complacency, nor rewarded by
their bounty.   His was a mightier protection, his a surer and
a higher destiny, and his is a more ample reward.   His is a
reward equivalent to his services, and his merits, and commen-
surate with the most exemplary virtue, the loftiest heroism, and
the profoundest wisdom.   The Greeks and Trojans live in the
songs of Homer and the poets, but Washington lives in the
heart of the World.   I only thus mention them with him to
show the superiority of his endowments, the greater justice of
his cause, and particularly to recognize the truer divinity that
shaped his ends, and is still directing the course of those
fortunes, which are the common heritage of freedom.   The
biography of Washington is being written.   "HE STILL LIVES."
His life is the round of the eternal ages, and as time rolls on,
each day, each year, each century will enhance his fame.   But
it is not too soon even now, to assert his superiority over all
other men of either ancient or modern times, for his opportunities and his splendid success, resulting from an almost

perfectly balanced mind, which makes the true man, already bespeak for him the highest place on the roll of fame. If we interrogate the world upon the subject, we shall find Washington already the occupant of the minds of men, and there are few who will venture to deny him the place which he occupies by almost universal acclamation. There have lived a few men whom to compare with Washington were not irreverence. But we shall find that though some warriors commanded greater armies, few have combined equal prudence and valor, and none have so united moderation with success. Among statesmen and rulers he stands without a rival, in the simplicity of virtue, in the majesty of wisdom, and in the perfection of his example. As a man he is a model which it is safe to copy, and if an overruling Providence presides over the affairs of men for their good, and is to be seen in outward manifestations, it would seem designed that by emulation of him men should be godlike.

HIS MORAL POWER.

It was the moral power of Washington, that bore him up against those waves of adversity that for a while overwhelmed his country. It was his moral power that struck with admiration the generous minds of other lands, and enlisted them under the banner of freedom, at that critical period of the revolution when the brave faltered and success was doubtful. It was his moral power that finally gave success to our arms, and by the magic of transmutation made the rebel the hero, the colonies states, and their federation the American Republic. By this power he withstood those temptations that ever surround the great, and so a crown was a bauble in his eyes, to be discarded as beneath the dignity of his nobler mind; as altogether too *common* a thing, and so he exhibits the anomaly of a man so great as to discard a thing so mean. His moral power gave the world confidence in our supposed experiment of self government, and has made it, so far, successful. Not that there have not been others who have played their part, and contributed to our success, and of whom we may speak, and of their characters and deeds, after we have exhausted the annals of the world in search of a man who can vie in true greatness and moral power with our own immortal Washington. But at the same time it is to be considered how far his character and example might have influenced even them, and whether success was probable or possible without the aid of his moral power.

HIS GREATNESS.

Certain it is that Washington is not greatest as a warrior, but as a man. I mean not as compared with others, but himself; for while he has not been excelled in heroism, he has not been equaled in individual excellence. So, while we institute comparisons between him and the great commanders of the world, it is more with the expectation of showing his superiority in those combined elements which secure ultimate success, than with the hope of finding, in the department of arms, a character the nearest parallel to his. The character of Cromwell illustrates this. Cromwell is the Englishman who is most like Washington, because he also is not greatest as a warrior, and because he is like him in success.

It is fortunate for the cause of peace and humanity that this is true. It is fortunate that the character of Washington, which occupies the highest place in the estimation of mankind, is not to be judged by those sanguinary qualities which are, in different degrees, the common elements of human nature, but rather by those higher endowments of mind which hold in subjection the ruder passions of ambition, pride and vain glory, and submit them to the test and arbitrament of reason. Herein consists the true greatness of Washington. It is not a perfect equilibrium of the faculties, but that near approximation to it, which, recognizing the economy of nature in the presence of all the human faculties, shows a predominance of intellectuality and moral power over those grosser functions which prompt mankind to feats in arms. Wherever this predominance of moral power is wanting, there we find a badly balanced mind, and it is sure to be displayed in individual action.

ALEXANDER THE GREAT.

We may give to Alexander the general praise of universal genius and empire, and descending to the incidental glories of such achievements as the battles of the Granicus. of Issus and Arbela, and the siege of Tyre; his magnanimity towards the mother, wife and daughters of Darius, when they were his captives, and found his camp a sacred asylum for their virtue; and his generosity to king Porus, in restoring to him his kingdom; we may accord to him the possession of the soul of chivalry, the fire of ambition, the love of glory, and the truthfulness of friendship, when friendship subserved his purposes, and was not in the way of his ambition. But did he not murder Clitus, in a debauch, for praising Philip, his father? Did he not treacherously assassinate the venerable and heroic Parmineo. the friend of Aristotle, his preceptor, to escape the consequences of having tortured and murdered his son Philotus upon mere suspicion? Did he not torture and murder Calisthenes? Did he not, at the suggestion of a courtesan, play the incendiary by setting fire to the palace of Darius with his own hands? And indeed, were not his military achievements as much the result of the weakness and imbecility of those he conquered as of his own efforts? What was he, in fact, but a great public murderer, plunderer and robber? And did he not die in youth, and a debauchee? What heroism, what magnanimity, what military genius, can atone for this? He must have derived his ideas of morality from his father, Philip, who discarded Olymphia, the mother of Alexander, and his own proper wife, *not for her physical inability to provide him with a son and worthy successor*, who existed in the person of

Alexander himself, but for the enrapturing charms of the more youthful Cleopatra.

Here then we naturally glide into a comparison, as by accident, to illustrate a principle, wherein the great Alexander must occupy a niche in the temple of fame how very far beneath the pedestal on which stands the father of our country! And more forcibly to show the effects of the moral power of these two great men upon the empires they established, and upon the world, let us see what cause they were severally engaged in, and what followed when they left the stage of action.

The empire of Alexander, a consolidated despotism, vast as it was, possessed no cohesive power of perpetuation, and scattered like a rope of sand. He did not foster, nor did his example encourage in his cotemporaries and successors, a spirit of emulation, which would incite them to become great rulers. He could bear no rival. He was jealous even of the fame of his own father, and murdered the man who had rescued him from death, and who was his best friend, for daring to do justice to the fame of Philip. The cause he was engaged in was that of his own selfishness. His incentive to action was his inordinate ambition, to satisfy which, even the spoils of the East and the subjugation of the world were inadequate. He claimed immortality, and slew those who were too sincere to pay him divine honors. His fame, therefore, has more of *quantity* than *quality* about it.

HE IS CONTRASTED WITH WASHINGTON.

On the other hand, Washington engaged in an unequal contest to rescue from the grasp of oppression the then infant colonies of America. It is not probable that, at that time, the splendid vision of the future of these United States had unveiled itself even to the most hopeful mind. The redress of wrongs then existing, and possible independence of the mother country, was about all that was looked for. Washington had no hope of spoils; he had no rich and populous cities to tempt him to plunder; he had no victorious legions who for an age had whetted their invincible swords against Roman or Persian shields, but a sparsely populated country, with a few small cities and villages which it was his duty to protect, and an army of rural peasantry unskilled in war, who had gathered at their country's call, and stood ready for those manipulations of the science of war which alone could qualify them for success. To join himself to the fortunes of the coming struggle, he must turn traitor to his king, and if not successful, sacrifice an honorable name for the opprobrium of a rebel, and perhaps come to a traitor's doom. Besides, look at the power that would oppose him : a nation whose diplomacy and arms had been the envy and terror of Europe and Asia for six hundred years ; whose navies rode the oceans in triumph, and whose traffickers, adventurers and emissaries had gathered into the lap of Britannia the garnered wealth of the East, and subjected the wilds of America to the uncontrolled range of the British lion ; thus, in effect, monopolizing the accumulated wealth of antiquity, and appropriating, in the acquisitions of Columbus, these splendid domains, which were fated to become the theatre and focus of a higher civilization, and holding the supremacy of commerce, become the arbiter in deciding the political destinies of the world.

WASHINGTON'S INSPIRATION.

For a man with such slender resources at his command, and so little inducement in the prospect of success, to assume the position of leader in a rebellion against the then colossal power of England, was an act wherein rashness and heroism seemed blended, and none but a mind indued with the spirit of prophecy could have prompted to such action the heart and arm of a hero.

HIS WISDOM.

Passing over those incidents of the conflict which are the
common topics of history, we are next to consider Washington,
when complete success had crowned him as a commander,
taking the helm of state. Disdaining proffered royalty, he
becomes the servant of the people, and as the first popular
magistrate of the American Republic, co-operating with
Franklin, Jefferson, Payne, and Adams, and the other sages
and patriots of his time, (himself the chief among them, by
common acclamation,) proceeds to put in motion this mighty
phenomenon of government, wherein the PEOPLE rule by
RIGHT DIVINE. His was the model administration of this
Republic. His example in office, and on leaving it, refusing
all remuneration for his services, satisfied with honor and
glory, rather than the avails of avarice; the stable basis upon
which he established the precedents of our democratic admin-
istrative function; his knowledge of national and international
law, of state and federal sovereignty, of the relative powers
and prerogatives of the several departments of the government
under the constitution, (never forgetting that the people are the
source of all power,) are evidences of his elevated and disinter-
ested patriotism, and of his superiority as a ruler. His advice
to his countrymen, when he bid them farewell, was the advice
of a father to his children, and can never be contemplated
without deep emotion. If his advice were listened to and
obeyed, the American Republic would be perpetual.

RESULTS OF HIS CAREER.

Of the results of the career of Washington, and his moral
influence on his country and the world, it is not fitting to
speak in comparison with those of Alexander. No parallel
can be drawn here, as there is no analogy. But upon those
results, incomparable as they are, it is proper to dilate,
briefly, in order to establish a criterion by which to judge

of others, who are supposed to have some claim to a similar influence.

WASHINGTON'S RETIREMENT AND DEATH.

Sixty-nine years have elapsed since Washington retired from the service of his country. That event brought tears to the eyes of the sages and heroes who surrounded him, and sadness and gloom over the whole country. At his death, two years later, a wail of lamentation rose to heaven from every mountain and valley and plain of this broad land, and funereal honors were done him in every city, village, town and hamlet of his redeemed country. The sorrow of his own countrymen was heartfelt and sincere, and many a noble soul in Europe paid the homage of tears to the manes of him who had extorted their admiration by his deeds, and their love and veneration by his godlike example. His departure filled the world with gloom, as though the sun had set, for his fame had gone abroad over the world wherever the flag of his country floated, and the children of Confucius, and Osiris, of Zoroaster and Mahomet, were touched in unison at the grief of the children of Washington!

THE NEW ERA.

Since that event, we behold the most astonishing changes in the affairs of the world and of this Republic. The morning sun of freedom, advancing toward the meridian, has warmed into life the before slumbering but latent energies of the human mind, and free thought and inventive skill have invaded the domain of the hitherto unknown, and brought from thence the spoils of industry and the glittering gems of intellect, as a grateful tribute due to the genius of liberty. While Franklin had evoked the spirit of the skies to inaugurate the dominion of freedom, Fulton bid the spirit of the waters speed the gliding train of commerce over land and sea,

2

and Morse, with magic hand, has bound in the eternal spell of omnipresence the thoughts of men, and made our name immortal. Again, we invade the realm of Neptune to establish a highway upon which thought shall travel, and now we hold a truce with the sovereign of the deep, till he reluctantly yields to freedom the right of way across the bottom of the Atlantic.

PROGRESS OF THE REPUBLIC.

Look at our progress in invention ; our arms, our printing presses, our locomotives and implements of agriculture, and various appliances of mechanism to the arts of civilization and the pursuits of domestic life, carried over the oceans in our ships to supply foreign lands. Look at their use here, and the result our supremacy in commerce. Look at our widening domain, magnified by honorable terms of accession, by purchase, by treaty, and by unwilling conquest. See a thousand cities rising upon it, and the world flocking to our shores, emulous to illustrate the principles and obey the precepts of Washington. See, even the tomb of Washington an object of profound regard ; the Mecca of the pilgrims of freedom, watched over by the daughters of Columbia, as the tomb of Jesus was watched over by the daughters of Palestine ; and see ! the first scholars and orators of the Republic cover the land with eulogies to adorn his tomb ! Is he not immortal ? and if he be not a god, is it for lack of the veneration paid to a god ? Witness the silent reverence of mankind at the mention of his name. Among men there is no name so sacred, except the name of God himself. We even see men scoff at religion, reject revelation and everything else sacred, but they tremble at the name of Washington as though it were the sign of omnipotence, and they dare not pass it. Truly, our sectaries have but a slender hold on the minds of men, compared with this !

These are the results that follow the career of Washington. Such is he, and such the grandeur of his fame. Need we go back to inquire if he be equal to Alexander? Let us rather hold up the laurels of a Xenophon, a Xerxes, a Pericles, a Numa, a Hannibal, a Scipio, a Fabius, an **Attila**, a Cæsar, an Alfred, a Frederick and Peter the Great, a Charles of Sweden, a Charlemagne and a Napoleon, and see them wither beneath the noonday glories of the fame of Washington!

XENOPHON.

I mention Xenophon, the Athenian, first, because he was not only a great commander, but an historian, a philosopher and sage, combining in himself the elements of real greatness; and great he was, though not faultless. He was the friend and disciple of Socrates, but, against the earnest entreaties of his preceptor, he listened to the claims of friendship, and the promptings of ambition, and was induced by Proxenus to join the expedition of Cyrus against his brother Artaxerxes, which proved disastrous, and the result was that after their total defeat in the battle of Cunaxa, by the army of Artaxerxes, Xenophon with ten thousand Greeks was compelled to flee six hundred leagues, and this flight, inglorious as it was, is called the retreat of Xenophon. For his skill in conducting this retreat, which is the most notable in ancient history, he has justly received all due praise; but had he been less ambitious, or had he listened to the wise counsel of Socrates, he would have escaped the glory and the shame of the expedition, and saved himself from the consequent disgrace of his subsequent public banishment from Athens. And what compensation had he for his glorious deeds in the service of Agesilaus, the Spartan king in Asia, or even for his part in the celebrated battle of Coronea, when his banishment took place afterwards, and since he died in exile?

XERXES.

What glory had Xerxes, the Persian king, in his army of more than five millions of human beings, when he could be defied at Thermopylæ by a band of three hundred heroic Spartans under Leonidas, or what substantial fortunes, or extent of dominion, could compensate for his debaucheries, his pride and insolence, which resulted in his assassination? He might bore a tunnel through Mount Athos, and see his fleet sail through it; he could throw chains into the ocean, to deride old Neptune for destroying his bridge of boats, and lash the waves with a whip for their seeming contempt of his egotism, but he has failed to satisfy the world of his title to true fame. Who would commit so great an outrage as to mention the name of Xerxes as the peer of Washington?

PERICLES.

Pericles, a name, the synonym of ancient Grecian civic and military renown, in statesmanship, oratory, military astuteness, and executive dignity unrivaled, illustrates the genius of an age without its wisdom, and a noble race without its virtue. He lessened the power of the Areophegus to enhance his own. At the mention of the name of Aspasia, the name of Pericles loses its lustre, and its greatness is transformed from a mountain of gold to a mountain of stone, which may indeed exist through interminable ages, and defy the elements of destruction, but without the celestial halo of moral beauty, or the resplendent rays of virtue to adorn its cloud capt summit.

NUMA.

Numa could not, like Washington, refuse a crown, and accepted it, whether willingly or with reluctance, and if he calmed the ferocity of the primitive Romans, he was the patron of *caste*, and as the exemplar of regal beneficence became the model, par excellence, of monarchical toleration, and by rendering monarchy plausible, was the more dangerous and formidable foe to human equality. He was, like the modern English Constitution, so fascinating an apologist of monarchy as to become the most insidious and dangerous enemy of human freedom.

HANNIBAL.

Of Hannibal, the Carthagenian, it may be acknowledged, that his military exploits equal those of any other general, notwithstanding his final defeat, his misfortunes and his *suicide*. His early victories in Spain ; his simultaneous marching of three great armies into Africa, Spain and Italy, and his triumph at Cannæ, are models of military strategy, bravery and success, which were the study of Napoleon, and it required the highest deliberation of the Roman Senate, assisted by the wise counsel of their ablest generals, to circumvent him, and by carrying the war into Africa, transfer the seat of war, and drive Hannibal from the gates of Rome. It was not to be expected that the genius of one man could outweigh the solid wisdom of the Roman Senate, touching war and conquest, and overreach the conceptions of a Scipio by superior military sagacity, and so the battle of Zama was fought, the Romans triumphed, and the military career of Hannibal was ended. His name is illustrious as a warrior, though his career was transitory, and his fall signal as that of Carthage itself.

THE SCIPIOS.

As for the Scipios, whether we prefer him who conquered Hannibal, or him who burned Carthage, the elder or the younger Africanus, let it not be forgotten that the former suffered by the ingratitude of his country, and died in obscurity, and the latter, as the instrument of Roman jealousy and revenge, destroyed with vandal fury the commercial metropolis of the world, weeping prophetic tears at the anticipation that a

like calamity would befall his own native city at a future age,
and that he died by violence, being strangled in his bed.
They were amongst the wisest counselors and most successful
generals Rome ever produced, and posterity has paid the debt
which their contemporaries owed to their fame, but it is to be
considered, whether their opportunities, or their exploits, even
if blest with the approbation of their country, could by any
means have made them the equals of Washington.

FABIUS.

Some have compared Fabius to Washington in prudence,
or rather, precaution. They may have resembled each other
in that respect, but in that only, and for which Fabius was
accused of cowardice, but Washington was praised as wise.
It was the time and *manner* of their precaution that made all
the difference.

AURELIAN.

Aurelian, the very prince of austerity, violence and cruelty,
whose valor could make Rome glorious, while his severity
rendered himself infamous, expiated the wrongs he had in-
flicted upon others through that vengeance they had learned
of himself, and his assassination, by his own soldiers, proved
that they loved liberty and hated despotism, and that they
hated slavery more than they loved military renown or Roman
grandeur. His was the first diadem of Rome, but it was
tarnished by his cruelties. He could triumph over Zenobia,
the Iberian queen, though she commanded an army of seven
hundred thousand men, but he could not triumph over his
own passions, and therefore he became the victim of revenge.

MILTIADES.

Miltiades, the glorious hero of Marathon, and master of the
Thracian Chersonesus, was found guilty of treason and con-

demned to death for raising the siege of Paros. He became
suddenly panic-stricken and overawed by the Persian power
which he had before trampled upon and defied; as though his
mind fluctuated betwixt ambition and fear, and his vacillation
was mistaken for treachery, and punished as crime, when it
was a consequence merely of his constitutional frailties. He
died in prison, and his corpse was ransomed by his son, to save
him from worse than a plebeian burial.

ATTILA.

Shall we mention the name of Attila, the fierce Hun, "the
scourge of God," as worthy of our regard? Roman malice
and detraction must have damaged this great favorite of his
people, who gashed their faces with knives and shrieked in
agony when he died. They buried him in a triple coffin of
gold and silver and iron, and turning the river from its channel,
buried him there, that the returning waves might shield from
desecration his precious dust, and then slew those who buried
him, that his sacred place of rest should be forever hidden
from the knowledge of men. His was the fierce spirit of
vengeance, sent by the Almighty to do His bidding, whom
Leo supplicated to save Rome, and ransomed her with his
tears, as before she had been ransomed from the iron grasp
of an Alaric, with the ill-gotten spoils of ecclesiastical plunder.
This surely is the antipode of the spirit of Washington, whose
milder aspect is the symbol of the celestial attribute of love.
And when we consider the career of the warlike Hun, and the
desolation that followed in his train, we are forced to acknowl-
edge that though the Almighty is a God of love, he is a God
of vengeance too. And shall we say that this Attila, who so
commanded the homage of his people, whose soul was theirs,
and whose inspiration rendered them invincible, does not, at
least in this, as well as in the homage paid him, resemble
Washington? There is many a Christian hero among the

warlike conservators of our modern civilization who resembles
Washington less, and who is not so godlike as he. His name
must have been aspersed, for unmitigated vice could never
have so fascinated his people, nor wickedness so entirely command their veneration.

JULIUS CÆSAR.

But of Cæsar, the great master of the world when Rome
was its mistress, what shall we say of him, in this comparison?
If greatness of character were not a QUALITY, as well as a thing
of magnitude, it is probable that the name of Julius Cæsar
would stand by the side of Washington's on the roll of fame;
but as the one is only great, while the other is good as well as
great, we take it that our Model Man is greatest as well as
best: because, in morals, goodness magnifies greatness, and
makes it more obvious. We can see bright objects farthest,
and the lustre that adorns the name of Washington makes
him the more obvious. We can see bright objects farthest,
and the lustre that adorns the name of Washington in his
exalted sphere, makes him the pole-star of the present and
the future; ever obvious, ever the same, ever great, though
his distance from other known and familiar objects prevents
his being measured, so that his magnitude and distance, if
not beyond imagination, are at least beyond demonstration.
Julius Cæsar is the Orion of the constellations, whose grandeur
and magnificence astonish the beholder; but he rises in March
and sets in June; while Washington, like the great luminary,
that is not the pole, but so near as to guide to it, shines
throughout the year of eternity. To make the figure perfect,
it is necessary to add, that the pole itself is infinite perfection.

CHARLEMAGNE.

If it is not too great a transition to stoop from these high
historical contemplations, let us now descend to the eighth

century of the Christian era, to touch briefly upon the character of Charlemagne. Though the founder of a dynasty which lasted near five hundred years, he was so ignorant that he could not even write his own name and yet he is claimed as the patron and restorer of learning. This seems paradoxical, but it is not more so than his reputed kindness and humanity, when attempted to be justified with his cruelty to the Saxons, of whom he butchered four thousand deliberately, and in cold blood, in a single day. But due allowance will, of course, be made for this sanguinary quality in him, when it is remembered that he did this to establish Christianity. What indeed was the slaughter of a few thousand rebels for the sake of establishing the celestial dominion of the Prince of Peace? He ravaged their country with fire and sword, and at last compelled their submission to Christianity. Of course he was not exactly like Washington, though he resembled him so far that, whereas Charlemagne established Christianity and his own dominion, Washington established universal toleration and the dominion of freedom.

ALFRED THE GREAT.

Alfred the Great, of England, is one of the names which it is proper to mention in this comparison, and it follows next in order of time.

Although, as we have said, Cromwell is the Englishman who most resembles Washington, still there is a certain aristocratical influence forever exerted in England in favor of monarchy, and by which, for paucity of numbers in individual greatness among their rulers, occasioned by the overwhelming power of their oligarchies, the name of Alfred is magnified, and also, from political motives with the legitimists, it has gained precedence in greatness over that of Cromwell. The latter being a plebeian king, and filling the *hiatus* in the rule of legitimate royalty occasioned by the execution of Charles the first; being, in a manner, a rebel and usurper, has ever since been an object of royal hatred, and hence it has followed, that as they could not deny the greatness of Cromwell, it has been necessary to magnify that of Alfred. He is therefore extolled for acts not his own, and his greatness is exaggerated to make him a successful competitor for greatness with the greater Cromwell. He is represented as an eminent law-giver, when in truth most of the laws he promulgated were framed by Ina, his predecessor, or borrowed from the Trojan and Grecian codes. These laws, fifty-two in number, form the basis, it is true, of English jurisprudence; but we are only to give Alfred credit for that which is his own, not for appropriating to his own use and convenience the ideas of others, which with English monarchists may indeed seem a virtue, but we will none of it.

Alfred fought fifty-six battles to conquer a peace, because he loved peace better than war. The suggestion seems imminent that he must have gotten bravely over his peace loving propensities before his wars were ended. And there may be some just and proper appreciation of his perseverance, when it is known that he was overpowered, conquered and driven into obscurity by the Danes, who at that time infested England, and but for the success in battle of the earl Odun, he could never have been induced to resume his royal prerogative. Here Alfred's greatness, as a king, depended upon Odun. It is mentioned as one of his exploits, for which he received much praise, that in the character of an harper he entered the camp of the enemy *as a spy*, and by that means gained some success. How would it look in Washington's military career if we should see him assume the character of a mountebank and a spy to gain success? There is a majesty, a sincerity, a dignity about the character of Washington, which forbids the idea of his being capable of such low cunning and deception. I do not say that Alfred is destitute of character as one of the great, but that his greatness has been magnified, and he has no right to stand betwixt Cromwell and the sun, because his shadow is too small to obscure him, much less is he the equal of Washington.

CROMWELL.

But can it be claimed that Cromwell himself is the equal of Washington? Did he possess the even balance of mind; the equilibrium of the moral, intellectual and physical powers so eminently constituting the MANLY STATUS of our Model Man? Are there not incidents in his life which disclose the predominance of physical power over moral and even intellectual power in this great man? Was he not severe beyond the exigencies of the times in which he lived? Did he aim sufficiently high to match his impelling force? These are questions which I will not presume to answer, but leave for solution by those who will hereafter decide with unbiased judgment, when the muse of history is not longer confronted by the spirit of mammon, nor shocked by the apprehension that liberty may be turned into license.

In his age and position, Cromwell surely represented the genius and power of a race of men in whose hands then rested the fate of human freedom. The conservative minds of his nation, even to this day, by virtue of his audacity and their own innate sense of justice and true perception of individual right, hold in check the power of the mob, the oligarchy and the throne. The Democracy of England is the genius of her Cromwell piercing through the mask of a superficial loyalty, and asserting, in defiance of royal or aristocratic prerogative, the rights of man. But with Cromwell did not end that hideous system of inequality which holds the many subject to the few; their laws of entail and primogeniture (relics of feudal barbarism) still remain. These must either be worn away by reformatory processes, or if delayed too long, be swept to oblivion by the angry wave of political revolution. Happy would it be for England, if the mind that rules her were so pervaded by the spirit of our advancing civilization as to discard, in time, those principles of injustice and wrong which sap the foundations of a political system founded in constitutional freedom. Here is the great antagonism that threatens the overthrow of her political liberties. It is the cause of all those social agitations which have shaken the British empire to its foundations, and constitutes and perpetuates an irrepressible conflict between popular liberty and diabolical despotism.

Cromwell arose on the tide of English civilization, and until the subsidence of that tide he occupies the crest of its topmost wave. A Shakspeare, a Bacon, a Milton, a Newton, may grace the temple of the ideal, but the colossal form of a Cromwell fills the highest place in the sphere of action, and brightens the glory and enhances the fame of England.

CHARLES OF SWEDEN.

Nine hundred years after Alfred, history records two illustrious names which should be more than mentioned, especially as one of them founded a mighty empire; for in this he was like Washington. These are the names of Charles of Sweden, who fought sixty pitched battles and was then killed by a cannon ball, and Peter the Great of Russia, whose dynasty still exists, as the great absolute antagonism of our republican form of government. These are great in quantity, and, it must be confessed, to a certain degree, good in quality also. Living contemporaneously, it is almost impossible to mention one without the other, though in respect to the consequences which resulted from their lives, it would be safe to select the character of Peter the Great as most suitable to compare with that of the founder of our government. And yet the heroism and success of Charles the twelfth, and that superiority of soul

that scorned the bauble of a crown, and arose above the allure-
ments of common greatness to the dignity of true manhood,
challenge the admiration of the world, and seal his name with
the impress of immortality.

PETER THE GREAT.

And of Peter the Great and his stupendous plans of empire;
plans which were conceived in prophetic reverie, and executed
with godlike energy, with an energy inherent in a noble race
of rulers, who derived their moral power from this illustrious
head, and seemed, by inspiration, the means adapted to the
end for carrying out the grand conceptions of the master
mind; of these it is just and proper briefly to speak with that
respect which the sublimity and the grandeur of the subject
inspire. Indeed, aside from the peculiar forms of government
which they established, and the political principles involved
therein, there is more similarity between the characters of
Washington and the Russian tzar than often occurs among
those so great. The Russian was virtuous and wise; so was
the American. He had industry and perseverance; so had
Washington. He was successful; so was Washington. He
was the model man and the model ruler of his nation; so
was Washington. The systems and governments they established, though political antipodes, are both successful and still
exist. They established two mighty empires, each of which
goes on increasing in extent, population and improvement.
Each of the men is called, and is the father of his country,
and they are alike objects of just veneration. But in the
estimation of mankind, since human nature is so constituted
as to love freedom, Washington is the best model, and would
be preferred, even if he did not excel Peter the Great in the
original constituent elements of human character. They may
yet be judged adversely, if in the future liberty should lose its
charm, by degenerating into mere license, and when patriotism

is but a name, and freedom a mask for oppression. But while
men love liberty, and are worthy of it by virtue of their intel_
ligence, and preserve it by the power of their wisdom, they will
esteem Washington as much higher than Peter the Great, as
they esteem democracy higher than monarchy.

NAPOLEON.

It now remains to us to compare our model man with
Napoleon Buonaparte. This is difficult because we find in
Napoleon those prominent qualities which we have already
described in others. He was a military and political eclectic.
In him we have the Alexander of our own age. In ambition
he was like Alexander, and not like Washington. Alexander
was one of the models which he studied, and although profuse
of originality, and possessed of abundant resources of his own,
he appears to have copied somewhat from the great masters of
his art. I would not call him a military plagiarist, but his
crossing the Alps was not an original idea, though an old one
well appropriated. That idea belonged to Hannibal. His
retreat from Russia was not as well conducted as the retreat
of Xenophon; it was a bad imitation. His great error was in
retreating at all. Why attempt impossibilities? Why demand
of his heroic army its own immolation? By adding exposure
to want, he decimated and almost annihilated his otherwise
invincible legions. He was surrounded by the resources of a
great empire, and was not beyond the reach of succor from
his own, when a little time would have elapsed and the face of
nature changed. Whatever may be said of his incidental
errors, this retreat was the capital error of his military career,
as the sundering of his domestic ties for purposes of ambition
was his capital political error. Both acts lost him the confidence of his soldiers and the people, and robbed him of self-
confidence. All his military prestige vanished, when his army
beheld him transformed from an invincible hero to a fleeing

fugitive. His own soul forsook him when he turned traitor to nature's law and false to his own natural affections, by discarding Josephine, the good angel, who had been with him in all his dreams of glory. But still he was our Alexander, and like him is scarcely to be compared to Washington. He is conceived, but not born of immortality, being blasted in the womb of time! His greatness is so irregular that it fails in continuity, and defies admiration. His deeds are mighty, but like the pillars of an unfinished temple, they are detached and mournful monuments of impracticable designs. They look like the ruins of Persepolis, but as they never constituted a whole, we are to consider them as the creations of one who was *a designer of ruins!*

This irregularity of greatness in the character of Napoleon, is being copied by the French nation. To-day they are a nation of freemen; to-morrow they are a nation of slaves. Once they had an excess of liberty, now they have none. They alternately rise to the heights of civilization, and sink to the depths of barbarism. They are either governed too much or too little. The massacre of St. Bartholomew, the corruption and effeminacy of the reign of Louis the 14th, the revolution of 1798, the epoch of Napoleon the 1st, and the *coup d'etat* of 1848, constitute the great facts of French history, and overshadow all the good government and march of improvement in the life of the nation.

The possibility of the recurrence of such historical enormities, such social cataclysms, such political transitions, such religious abnegations, is too horrible to contemplate, from which the nation is only redeemed by the countervailing element of an indestructible, indomitable, though latent spirit of Democracy.

The accession to power of the present French ruler, proves the veneration of the French people for the character of Napoleon, without which they might have shown more continuity of freedom, but the existence of that veneration is hostile to the idea of freedom. And what are the results of the career of Napoleon? His successor was placed upon the throne of France by the suf-

frages of the combined monarchies of Europe, by which France,
in effect, lost her sovereignty and self-control. That monarch,
sustained by foreign bayonets, maintained a precarious show of
existence and power, (fortunately escaping repeated attempts at
his assassination until the period of 1848,) when he vanished
like a spectre from the presence of the majestic ghost of Euro-
pean revolution. Then came the brief respite of *Liberty, Equality* and *Fraternity*, and France was free and happy as a Republic. How brief, how transitory, was her joy! For lo! the hideous phantom of Empire broke her peaceful slumber; her para-
disal dream of bliss dissolved and vanished in the delusive moon-
light haze of military glory, and the mighty soul which took its
exit from St. Helena had returned and hovered over France.
Behold the "man of destiny," the *protege* of ecclesiastical cunning, the "*protector of holy places*" raised to the imperial dignity by the force of mere military reminiscence, and by a super-
stitious and farcical assumption of the chimera that the god-like
soul of a Napoleon could become the inhabitant of that lillipu-
tian mind. So hath France bartered her liberties for a phantom,
and obscured the glories of her brightest epoch by this prepos-
terous substitution of a pigmy for a giant, who hides his littleness
and deformity behind a cloud of Roman mist to shun the day-
beams of the star of Washington.

The present ruler of France has immersed himself in a black
cloud of moral turpitude of more than cimmerian darkness,
which cannot be illumed neither by the evanescent light of erra-
tic mind, the fire of ambition, nor the sickly glare of military
achievement and glory, (the death-pallor of civilization,) and
notwithstanding these may, with transient lustre beguile the awe-
struck nations, like the wandering, vagrant spectre of the skies,
their light is all too dim to penetrate the unfathomable abyss of
barbaric gloom into which he plunged when through perjury and
stratagem he won the goal of his ambition, and by perfidy be-
trayed the blood-bought suffrages of the French people; when

by usurpation he trampled upon the liberties of his country, by violence and aggression suppressed Roman freedom; by cupidity exiled the soul and intellect of France, and through cowardice shackled the free speech and the free press of a great nation. And is he not even now plying those potent engines of civilization against civilization, secretly to supplant freedom and equality, that he may establish a Napoleonic dynasty in succession, and build upon the ruins of a democratic civilization a consolidation of universal and perpetual despotism? The world knows this project, and it will prove an abortion.

And of what avail to French Monarchists or Imperialists are all their reveries of past, present or future military achievement? What though they be environed by the colossal power of confederated kings. Are not their bastard dynasties secretly spit upon by all the legitimists of Europe? Who are their allies as against the peace of the world, and in the extension of their unjust and ignoble dominion? Is Russia their ally since the destruction of Moscow, the *coup d'etat*, or the conspiracy of the Crimea? Is England suddenly their ally, after ten centuries of hostility, because of the superior *integrity* of the Imperial successor of the victim of St. Helena? Is Prussia their true ally, with her English alliance and religious antagonism? Is America their ally, while they exile freedom from their shores, and wield a shackled press to uphold despotism? Let not the mistaken idea of our former friendly alliance with France, which was mainly the result of her hostility to Great Britain, blind our eyes to the fact of her submission to-day to the reign of a usurper, who stamps on freedom with the iron heel of arbitrary power. Let not the admirers of the great Napoleon forget that wisdom is superior to genius, and if he had been wise, as he was brilliant and brave, our alliance might have been perpetual, yet then Napoleon would not have been the peer of Washington. But when we contemplate the great errors of Napoleon, and perceive in his nation to-day a ready submission to usurpation and wrong, for the purpose of

mere *grandeur*, how shall we admire greatness at the expense of
justice ; how ally ourselves to tyranny, or view with complacency
the triumph of violence, perjury and wrong?

The French nation, following their great copy, are an enigma
not now fully understood. Their idolatry of him looks like
devotion to despotism. And if we are to judge from the past
and consider the character of Napoleon as their model, is it not
strange that the enlightened and virtuous sovereign of Great
Britain should assume to unite in cordial companionship with
so portentous and uncertain a phenomenon?

This naturally leads the mind to a contemplation of the past,
and to the interrogation of the future :

ENGLAND.

Where are the empires that adorned the world
In time's dim vista? Where their haughty kings,
That glittered in the blaze of antique glory,
Whose renown eclipsed the sun of the ideal,
The eyes of the young world bedimmed with splendor,
And made romance a fable and a dream !
Where are their thrones, and palaces, and walls
With brazen gates, and towers of fretted gold,
And where those myriad throngs, that lived and toiled
To mark the greatness of their cruel kings;
That blew the trump of fame with folly breath
To ears of fools; that trode the verdant plains
To feats in arms, and won them fetters,
And whose deeds, emblazoned on their scrolls of fame,
Were writ on sand! Are they gone,
To make, and grace, and serve some airy court,
And have they followers too?

A throne there is, methinks, in this our day,
Of pride, and pomp, and great magnificence,
Where sits a beauteous queen, and her fair progeny,
Whose base shall totter in the coming wind

OF OTHERS.

To the foregoing may be added the names of Aristides, Cato, Cincinnatus and Socrates, Timoleon, Epaminondas, Augustus and Tamerlane, names illustrious in the annals of the world, and combining, like Washington, in an eminent degree, the united elements of heroism and statesmanship, and some of them eminent for their virtue and wisdom, as well as their valor and patriotism; but on account of the age or country in which they lived, or their smaller opportunities, no one of them, in character and action, in his career and its consequences, combined, can be claimed as the peer of Washington. Some men, claiming immortality while they lived, and endeavoring to extort by cruelty the unwilling homage of mankind, became infamous; others, by the rashness of desperation, enkindling enthusiasm, which they mistook for idolatry, became vain, and fell victims to austerity and pride; others, whose single excellences in some things rested under the shadow of a countervailing vice, were rather bad than good; others, in whom virtue and wisdom predominated, lavished their goodness on wicked or idolatrous generations, by whose ingratitude they were neglected, or by whose hostility they became prisoners or exiles.

ARISTIDES, the Just, was banished his country for ten years, by the influence of his rival, Themistocles, and though recalled from his banishment in six years, he died in poverty, and was buried by charity at Athens.

THEMISTOCLES was also an exile.

SOCRATES, with all his superior wisdom, exemplary virtue and heroism, gained, but could not hold, the veneration of his fellow-men. The wit, satire and ridicule of an Aristophanes proved too much for his influence among his contemporaries. He first lost his influence, and then his life, because his philosophy sounded beyond the depths of humanity in his time. It is doubtful if he would meet a better fate in our own age and country. But what wit, sophistry or ridicule could loosen the hold that Washington has upon his fellowmen? Genius would wither at the hostile touch of a hair of his sacred head!

TIMOLEON's hands are stained with the blood of his own brother! The avenger of his country's wrongs even at the sacrifice of a brother's life, because that brother attempted to seize power as a usurper by means of a *coup d'etat!* He protected the rights of the people even by such a sacrifice as this. Nature abhors the act, and truth and virtue tremble in the presence of such a benefactor. Who ever dreamed of venerating him, though his deeds were ever so meritorious?

CATO, the severe and rigid enemy of luxury, and even of refinement; the representative man of plebeian rudeness, manners, customs and habits; the opponent of learning, and lover of rudimental simplicity and physical superiority in man, even with all his prudence, primitive virtues and just dread of the effeminacy of Grecian refinement, was the victim of austerity, and therefore, as he was a just man, Virgil elevates him to a magistracy in Hell!

CINCINNATUS, with his sixteen days successful campaign, and twenty-one days dictatorship, flashes like a meteor athwart the sky of Roman action, and as an actor, eludes the grasp of the world's judgment, except in the obscurity of private virtue, where, with the million, he is secure from the glory and shame of common greatness, and the fickleness of fortune and of fame. He has not the advantage of the well tried and successful hero, or statesman, and is therefore far remote from Washington in the sphere of fame.

SOLOMON. It is without arrogance, therefore, that we proclaim the truth that Washington is a wiser and a greater man than Solomon. The march of civilization and human progress have changed the magnific status of the Jewish King. The moral brightness of his wisdom, reflected from the Orient, illumines none of these American States except *Utah* or Deseret, and since VIRTUE is the offspring of WISDOM, she now points exultingly to WASHINGTON as her favorite son.

THE ANNUNCIATION.

We turn, then, with reverence, to the father of our country, as the only MODEL which it is safe to copy, in ancient or modern times. Admonished of the fate of the projectors of new theologies and new philosophies, how they have ever encountered the hostility of bigots, the fury of fanaticism, and the scorn of conventional egotism, we here defer to the well known and established opinions and convictions of mankind (the spontaneous growth of unfettered and unrestrained wisdom) the annunciation of the dogma of the MODEL MAN; and while we claim to the behoof of reason the perception and the recognition of this standard erected by the divine hand, in view of man's aspiration to virtue, wisdom and heroism, we discard the vaguest conjecture of those prudes in piety, who can see only within the circle of their own narrow vision, that we here unqualifiedly reserve the act of *worship* and *adoration* as due to God alone. This MODEL is for man, as man, in this world, and is created and established by Providence as a higher physical and moral gradation to which mankind must ascend as they rise upward to the inheritance of eternal felicity.

Let us hasten, then, from these glimpses at the Sages and Heroes of antiquity, and contemplate briefly the character of Washington as

THE MODEL MAN.

The use of a model is to fashion others by it. The model should be faultless, because any defect in it is not only its own, but is impressed upon all that may be fashioned by it. There are many departments of industry, mechanism and art, wherein models are necessary, and often indispensable, and if in any piece of mechanism, a flaw, blemish or defect comes, from a defect in the model or pattern, such piece of mechanism, if adapted at all, in shape or fitness, to the purpose intended, will grate harshly, or snap, or retard the motion of the entire machine, or cause it sooner to wear out. The model, there-fore, is of great consequence, as it affects all that may be fashioned after it.

In the art of chirography also, for example, if the scholar have a defective copy, he will imitate the defects as well as the excellences in it, and make slow progress, because he first learns the defects, and must then unlearn them, which is the most difficult. But give him an engraved copy, or one written by one of those masters of the art, of whom there is but one in many millions, and his progress will be more rapid, and he will arrive at a higher degree of excellence.

THE IDEAL AND THE REAL.

It is said of great artists, those whose productions in marble were bought for their weight in gold, that they copied from nature those graces and charms which won for them the applause of men, and their fame was enduring, while those who copied from works of art, or gave inadequate delineations of the ideal, without due reference to the anatomy or natural conformation of grace and beauty, go with their works to oblivion. Who cannot tell a fancy sketch from a reality; the portraiture of a real man from an ideal one? Reality always has some distinctive marks and peculiarities about it, which ever elude the grasp of art in the ideal. Why are we often struck with certain forms of beauty in nature which surprise us? Is it not because they excel the conceptions of imagina-tion? Who has ever painted a real rainbow, or the glowing disc of the sun? Is nature's superiority over art not here well understood? Then shall we not interrogate nature, and shall we not in nature seek for our model, and finding, copy it?

THE BEAUTIES OF NATURE.

Nature is, indeed, filled with forms of beauty; with glowing gems, of divers shapes, and hues, and brilliancy; with painted blossoms, of gaudy colors, fairy forms and delightful odors; with forms animate, and of movement or locomotion diverse. Look at the insect tribes! With gilded wings and burnished limbs they flutter in the sunbeams! What various form, and motion, and action, in those that swim, and crawl, and travel, and fly, and think and reason and imagine! Millions of pliant fins dip the wave; millions of tiny feet touch the earth; millions of glittering wings flit in air; millions of monads listen to the roar of the zephyr, that stuns their tiny ears; millions of eyes behold the sun and dissect his rays; millions of fairy forms glide over earth and ocean; millions of angel faces are the mirrors of their souls; millions of human imaginations roam in the enchanted realms of ecstacy. But in all nature, amid the rare and the beautiful, the most wonderful of all is that rarest microcosm, the MODEL MAN.

The reason for this is his complex nature. He is. He lives. He moves. He thinks. He reasons. He imagines. He excels. He aspires. Of this gradation, from the inanimate to the intelligent, he is the apex, and head. Man's intellect is the crest of the wave that first kisses the sunlight of celestial beauty. But the distinctive character of the model man is expressed when we say, HE EXCELS. His then becomes the diffusive influence of the wave distilled in air, kissed by the sunlight, transported by the zephyrs, and imbibed by the flowerets of earth, becomes the spirit of their odors and perfumes!

His is not the excellence of mere genius, whereby the faculty of imagination, with certain accessories, leads forth the soul triumphant into the domain of the ideal. His is not the excellence of Reason, which, plodding wingless, in the concrete paths of materiality, discards the realm of the ideal, and the unknown, that domain of hope, whence comes all new knowledge. He has no excess of wings in his imagination, nor body in his reason, so he can both fly and travel with facility, being well poised. Hence, with his eyes open, he can see the fitness of wings to an angel, as well as of claws and teeth to a reptile. He sees the utility of the ideal as well as the real, and knows it is not created in vain. His excellence is not in the force of one faculty at the expense of another, but in all the human faculties in equilibrio. He becomes, then, the exponent of humanity, because he is the realization of God's idea of a man, and is therefore The MODEL. ✓

This is Washington. And this announcement may well startle the devotees of ancient theology, the worshipers of a plurality of gods, for this model is a new revelation of the will of heaven, which will smite to the dust the idols of their infidel theologies, by becoming a standard for mankind, as men, and instituting the worship of God alone.

VIOLATIONS OF THE ETERNAL LAW.

It has ever been the fault of mankind to violate the sacred laws of Deity, by endeavoring to break down the barrier which hides the Infinite from the vulgar gaze of mortals. The Persians, the Chinese, the Egyptians, and the Romans, all claimed to have their sacred Ambassadors at the court of Heaven, who not only enjoyed the honor of celestial intercourse, but actually usurped or shared the prerogatives of the Eternal. And it is well known that at each successive violation of the eternal law, there is more than one aspirant to the celestial office. The sacred barrier once broken down which bounds the aspiration of human ambition and human audacity, a mob of deities rushes in, and each claiming to be the favorite in the divine presence, arrogates to itself the powers and exercises the prerogatives of Deity.

The happy idea of a Model Man could not occur to the inventors of the antique theologies, because their purpose was to second, by their efforts, the assumed divine right of kings. They were their accessories, and as human equality was to them an undiscovered truth or a false dogma, their secondary deities could not be models for men to copy, for they were either the austere and arbitrary dispensers of kingly authority, the inimitable performers of miracles, or the sole executors of divine decrees. How could they, then, be models, since to copy them were impossible, and the attempt to do so an act of arrogance and irreligion?

OF DEMAND AND SUPPLY.

The sacred dogma of human equality creates the necessity for the MODEL MAN. It is one of the fixed principles of nature, that there shall be, somewhere, a supply for every want, and it will be found that when a want exists, its supply is not far off. So we see, as equality has become the fixed and ruling idea of our age, through the agency of the combined wisdom, and virtue, and valor of the sages who announced it, there exists, simultaneously with it, a high standard of individual excellence, which is a proper model to be copied by men, so that the standard of equality shall be high, and not low; so that the standard of manhood shall be a standard of virtue and not of vice, of wisdom and not of folly. The aspiration of man is to this excellence, and this is why we find the name of Washington held sacred in our time. This aspiration indicates the necessity which the MODEL MAN supplies, and the consolidation of the empire of freedom, its stability, its perpetuation, its immortality and glory, dictate the principle that its great archetype and model be deemed as of immortal and celestial origin.

This is not a church canonization, but a philosophical identification. It is not the discovery of a great truth, but its promulgation. Its discovery took place in the spontaneous homage paid to greatness, purity and truth, in the character of Washington. This is an idea which the church will shun, because it is a substitute for canonization, and an improvement upon it. Nor is it deification, but the perception of true manhood. To deify, implies the obligation to worship whomsoever is deified. But if we recognize but one God, worship is due to Him alone. It can be no act of impiety, then, while we adore the mighty Architect and Ruler of the universe, if we recognize in his providence this high standard of individual excellence, as erected by Him, to lift men to the elevated sphere of human equality.

Equality cannot exist on a low plane. It cannot exist in the sphere of vice and ignorance, for there man is ever a prey to tyranny. Besides, the very aspirations of man would disdain the ignoble sphere of vice, and cannot dwell therein, while the lowly look upward with admiration to the sublime sphere of virtue and wisdom, and strive, however humbly, to aspire to it. It will be seen, therefore, that there is a necessity for a high standard of equality in manhood, because it is adapted to the aspiration of all men. A low standard would be unsuitable and insufficient, because the aspirations of men would be continually rising above it.

ANALYSIS OF HIS CHARACTER.

The question naturally arises here, whether the character of Washington is so elevated as to become the MODEL. To which I answer, that if the veneration of mankind is not sufficient evidence of that fact, it will be found in a careful analysis of his character.

He was virtuous without vain glory.

He was brave without defiance.

He was wise without pedantry.

He was grave without austerity.

He was humble without self-abasement.

He was religious without superstition or bigotry.

He was earnest without enthusiasm.

He was sagacious without cunning.

He was exempt from conventional errors.

He was munificent without ostentation.

He was affable without levity.

He was serious without moroseness.

He was generous, but just.

He was exemplary without a fault.

He was temperate without abstinence.

He had no vices nor caprices.

He had opportunity equal to his capacity.

He had, therefore, passion guided by reason,

And energy controlled by judgment.

He was successful only according to his endeavors.

He did not perform miracles, nor violate the laws of his country.

He was not a peace man while his country was enslaved, nor for war against universal despotism while freedom was in its cradle.

His genius was not pointed nor local, but broad and universal. It had little of the flash of poetry about it, by which to create worlds out of nothing, but the intuition of mathematical precision, by which to create and fashion real things from pre-existing materials.

Behold the work of his hand! This free and mighty Republic is the best commentary upon the character of Washington, for without his moral influence it would have been another form of government. By his assent it might have been a military despotism, and himself its king. No one will deny this who has read history; none will deny to him the elements of character we have attributed to him, who has read and understood his history, for it constitutes the glory of our country's history, tradition, and our common fame. Where shall we find his equal? Not in the long, dark catalogue of kings. Their history is a record, mainly, of violence, injustice, wickedness and misfortune; of great opportunities lost, for the amelioration and elevation of their race: of the uniform repression of manly aspiration, healthful innovation, and useful invention. Not amidst the array and dazzle and effeminacy of princes, where virtue is often a stranger and wisdom seldom known. Not among the moral heroes, statesmen, philosophers and representative men whose errors and misfortunes we have briefly narrated. The most formidable rivals of his fame were, perhaps, among his own contemporaries and countrymen, but, even among them, there could be but one Washington.

If the character of Washington is unfit for a model, it is not because any have ever equaled him. If such a standard is too low, it is not because any one can reasonably hope to excel him. There is no danger or probability of his being excelled. An equilibrium of the human faculties in man is the ultimatum of his being, in this world. It is a condition that cannot be improved upon, and Washington approximated to that condition. It is the equilibrium of the human faculties which the wisdom of antiquity points to, when the lion and the lamb shall lie down together, and there shall be none to hurt nor destroy in all the holy mountain of the mind. The best guaranty of the permanence of human freedom is to be found in the unapproachable grandeur of his fame.

Hymn to Washington.

————•————

They hold a taper to the sun,
  And boast its glories near his shrine—
Who claim the palm for victories won,
  Or regal fame, compare with thine!

The gild of pride, the pomp of power,
  Like glittering insects, in thy rays,
Dissolve and vanish in an hour—
  But fame prolongs thy lengthened days.

Heroes and kings may deck the page
  With storied deeds and trophies bright,
And laureled bards in phrensy rage,
  Their transient honors to requite,

But FAME herself adorns thy brow
  With honors time can never fade,
And truth, eternally, as now,
  Shines forth in thy pure soul arrayed.

Why doth the sage thy deeds indite,
  And gather trophies round thy tomb?
Why weave his glowing chaplet bright,
  To deck that paradise of gloom?

What magic spell asserts its sway,
  To kindle in the souls of men
Blest visions of a brighter day?
  Ah! all shall meet as brothers then!

The golden epoch shall return,
  Peace guide the nations as of yore,
When man thy mission shall discern,
  And at the shrine of truth adore.

Look down, IMMORTAL! from thy car—
  The chariot of the sun restrain!
I hear thee whisper, from afar,
  The peaceful age shall come again.

ERRATUM.

In thirtieth line, page 5, read: "are found *in* just equipoise."

www.ingramcontent.com/pod-product-compliance
Lightning Source LLC
Chambersburg PA
CBHW030909260626
47169CB00008B/2756